KATIE WOO and PEDRO Mysteries

The Mystery of the Missing Moose

by Fran Manushkin

illustrated by Tammie Lyon

PICTURE WINDOW BOOKS
a capstone imprint

Published by Picture Window Books, an imprint of Capstone
1710 Roe Crest Drive, North Mankato, Minnesota 56003
capstonepub.com

Text copyright © 2024 by Fran Manushkin
Illustrations copyright © 2024 by Capstone

All rights reserved. No part of this publication may be reproduced in whole or in part, or stored in a retrieval system, or transmitted in any form or by any means, electronic, mechanical, photocopying, recording, or otherwise, without written permission of the publisher.

Library of Congress Cataloging-in-Publication Data
Names: Manushkin, Fran, author. | Lyon, Tammie, illustrator. | Manushkin, Fran. Katie Woo and Pedro mysteries.
Title: The mystery of the missing moose / by Fran Manushkin ; illustrated by Tammie Lyon.
Description: North Mankato, Minnesota : Picture Window Books, an imprint of Capstone, [2024] | Series: Katie Woo and Pedro mysteries | Audience: Ages 5-7. | Audience: Grades K-1. | Summary: When Pedro's favorite stuffie, Milo the Moose, goes missing at the fair, Katie and Pedro retrace their steps in order to solve the mystery.
Identifiers: LCCN 2023020983 (print) | LCCN 2023020984 (ebook) | ISBN 9781484688601 (hardcover) | ISBN 9781484688687 (paperback) | ISBN 9781484688595 (pdf) | ISBN 9781484688731 (kindle edition) | ISBN 9781484688694 (epub)
Subjects: LCSH: Woo, Katie (Fictitious character)—Juvenile fiction. | Chinese Americans—Juvenile fiction. | Hispanic Americans—Juvenile fiction. | Stuffed animals (Toys)—Juvenile fiction. | Soft toys—Juvenile fiction. | Lost articles—Juvenile fiction. | CYAC: Mystery and detective stories. | Chinese Americans—Fiction | Hispanic Americans—Fiction. | Soft toys—Fiction. | Lost and found possessions—Fiction. | LCGFT: Detective and mystery fiction.
Classification: LCC PZ7.M3195 Mwm 2024 (print) | LCC PZ7.M3195 (ebook) | DDC 813.54 [E]—dc23/eng/20230516
LC record available at https://lccn.loc.gov/2023020983
LC ebook record available at https://lccn.loc.gov/2023020984

Design Elements by Shutterstock: Darcraft, Magnia
Designed by Dina Her

Table of Contents

Chapter 1
A Trip to the Fair 5

Chapter 2
Milo Goes Missing 12

Chapter 3
Case Closed! 18

Chapter 1
A Trip to the Fair

Pedro and Katie were playing in Pedro's yard. Pedro had his moose, Milo, with him.

"There's a fair in town," said Pedro's dad. "Let's go get some great fair food."

"And play games," said

Pedro. "And go on lots of rides!"

"Let's go down the big slide," said Pedro's dad.

"It looks scary," said Pedro, "but fun!"

They climbed up, up, up, the slide. Then they slid down. Pedro held Milo tight.

Next they walked to the ring toss.

"I can do this!" said Pedro.

He tossed the ring one . . . two . . . three times!

He missed! Pedro did not win the big bear.

Katie told him, "Maybe we will have better luck if we play the balloon game. I want to win that big bear."

Katie threw six darts.

She missed! No prize for Katie.

Chapter 2
Milo Goes Missing

"It's time for ice cream," said Pedro's dad.

The ice cream was soft and sweet and drippy!

"I'm glad I didn't drip ice cream on Milo," said Pedro.

"You can't," said Katie.

"He's gone."

"Oh no!" said Pedro. "Where is he? Milo is my buddy! I can't sleep without him."

Katie thought and thought. "There are so many stuffed animal prizes at the fair," she said. "Maybe Milo got mixed up with them."

Was Milo at the cotton candy stand?

No! Only a lot of sticky hands and faces.

Chapter 3
Case Closed!

Pedro cried, "I will never find Milo!"

"Don't give up," said Katie. "He has to be somewhere. Moose do not just disappear!"

They walked to the big slide. They saw lots of kids sliding down. One girl had a moose! Was it Milo?

No! It was a smaller moose.

They ran to the balloon game. They saw someone wearing the same shirt as Milo. Was it Milo?

No! It was a girl playing the game.

Pedro's dad hugged Pedro. "Let's be detectives and retrace our steps. That is the best way to find Milo."

"Smart idea!" said Pedro. "The ring toss had a lot of bear and tiger prizes. Maybe they thought my moose was a prize and put him on the shelf?"

They ran to the ring toss.

Pedro saw bears!

And tigers!

And sitting on a high shelf—

A moose!

The owner gave Milo to Pedro.

"I was holding him for you! Some kids wanted to win him, but I said, 'No way! That moose is someone's friend.'"

"Thank you!" said Pedro.

"He is my best friend."

Pedro hugged Milo all the way home . . .

About the Author

Fran Manushkin is the author of Katie Woo, the highly acclaimed fan-favorite early-reader series, as well as the popular Pedro series. Her other books include *Happy in Our Skin*, *Plenty of Hugs!*, *Baby, Come Out!*, and the best-selling board books *Big Girl Panties* and *Big Boy Underpants*. There is a real Katie Woo: Fran's great-niece, but she doesn't get into as much trouble as the Katie in the books. Fran lives in New York City, three blocks from Central Park, where she can often be found bird-watching and daydreaming. She writes at her dining room table, without the help of her naughty cats, Goldy and Chaim.

About the Illustrator

Tammie Lyon, the illustrator of the Katie Woo and Pedro series, says that these characters are two of her favorites. Tammie has illustrated work for Disney, Scholastic, Simon and Schuster, Penguin, HarperCollins, and Amazon Publishing, to name a few. She is also an author/illustrator of her own stories. Her first picture book, *Olive and Snowflake*, was released to starred reviews from *Kirkus* and *School Library Journal*. Tammie lives in Cincinnati, Ohio, with her husband, Lee, and two dogs, Amos and Artie. She spends her days working in her home studio in the woods, surrounded by wildlife and, of course, two mostly-always-sleeping dogs.

Glossary

detective (dih-TEK-tiv)—a person who collects information to figure out what has happened in a crime or other problem

disappear (dis-uh-PEER)—to no longer exist or be seen

drippy (DRIP-ee)—tending to drip

retrace (ree-TRAYS)—to go over something, like a path or route, again

shelf (SHELF)—a long, narrow piece of material fastened to a wall to hold objects

All About Mysteries

A mystery is a story where the main characters must figure out a puzzle or solve a crime. Let's think about *The Mystery of the Missing Moose*.

Plot

In a mystery, the plot focuses on solving a problem. What is the problem in this story?

Clues

To solve a mystery, readers often look for clues. Did Pedro and Katie have any clues in this mystery?

Red Herrings

Red herrings are bad clues. They do not help solve the mystery. Sometimes they even make the mystery harder to solve. Were there any red herrings in this story? Explain your answer.

Thinking About the Story

1. How do you think Pedro felt when he realized Milo was missing? List some of the clues from the story that tell you how he felt.

2. If Pedro went to the fair the next day, do you think he would bring Milo along again? Explain your answer.

3. Have you ever been to a fair? What did you see there? What did you do, and what did you eat? Write a paragraph about your time there.

4. Do you have a special stuffed animal? Draw a picture of your favorite stuffie, and write a paragraph about it.

Detective Memory!

Detectives need to be good observers. That means they need to pay attention to the people and things around them. Use this memory game to practice your observation skills, so you are ready if you ever need to solve a case like *The Mystery of the Missing Moose*! At least two people are needed to play.

What you need:

- a large tray

- a variety of 15–20 small objects (All of the objects should fit on the tray.)

- a pen and paper for each detective

What you do:

1. One player, the presenter, presents the tray of items to the other players, who will be the detectives. The detectives can look at the tray of items for about 30 seconds.

2. The presenter takes the tray away, leaving it in another room. The detectives should then list on their paper all the items they saw on the tray.

3. The detective who lists the most correct items wins and becomes the presenter. If possible, use a new selection of small objects for the next round.

4. After you've all had turns being the presenter, try this: Instead of taking away the entire tray, take away only a few items from the tray. Can the detectives identify which items are missing?

Solve more mysteries with Katie and Pedro!

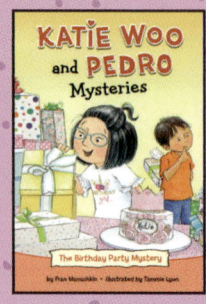
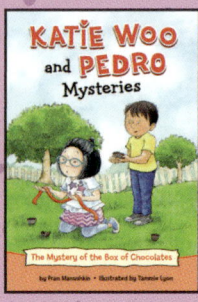
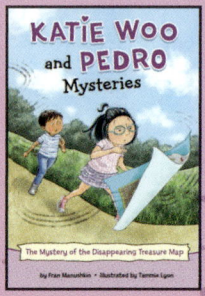
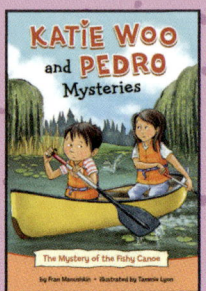
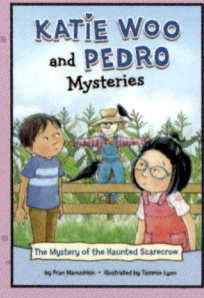
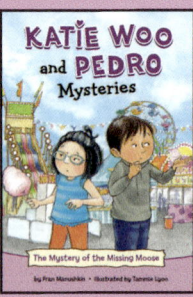

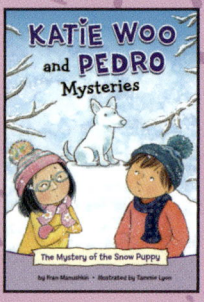
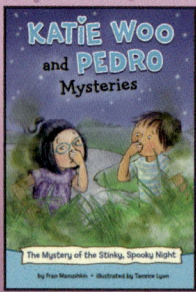
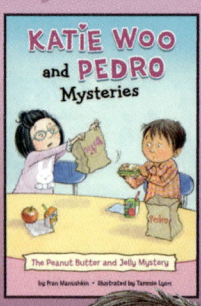
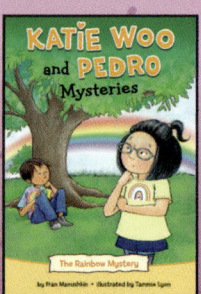
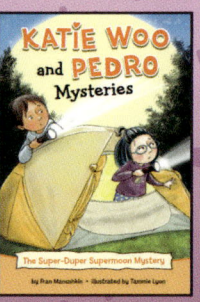